Limericks…

By Ernest Motion

A fair caddy master called Rob,
Rumour has it, he's worth a
few bob.
On the strength of a fart,
He'd recruit a new start,
Stating, "you're just the man
for the job."

Ernest Motion…

Limericks…

By Ernest Motion

Limericks …

By Ernest Motion

Do you fit into this category?
For enjoying, a short silly story.
You'll need a broad mind,
As the contents you'll find,
Are suitable for ADULTS ONLY.

18+

36 years in the baking

This book contains an antiquated historical style of adult humour, sexual content and potentially offensive use of language some readers may find upsetting-whereas others may revel in the honesty and observation contained in the following prose.

Executive Summary

1

For young Tommy Tourette had a grip,
No joy in just shouting out flip.
He'd cunt, fuck and laugh,
And yell, "Miss, suck me aff!",
On his primary two summer trip.

2

Halitosis was a problem for Chelle
And caused her breath to excessively smell.
Along with this challenge,
Was a pH imbalance,
Ensuring her fud stank as well.

3

Auntie Floss came to afternoon tea,
With a toy dog, her baby, Enri.
The randy, gas-filled young Pug,
Stank the parlour with fug
And humped shins, much to everyone's glee.

4

So, GRINDR, appealed to fat Stan,
No problem in getting his man.
With copious hair,
And a fart like a bear,
Drooling suitors, arrived soon, by van.

5

On their hol's, Ed and Flo felt dejected,
In the Hotel Dubai, quite neglected.
'Tween exotic birds sucking,
Noisy banging and fucking,
Not the calm desert break they'd expected.

6

An obsessional fellow named Jules,
Had a growing collection of stools.
Among the prized pieces,
Of catalogued faeces,
Were of Gran, armadillo and bull.

7

With rotting great fat plates of meat,
Bob was formerly proud of his feet.
Now with cuticle fails
And puff pastry toenails,
His podiatrist succumbed to defeat.

8

A penny tray sweetie piranha,
Was born into sugar Nirvana.
Her smile would cause grief,
With her puff candy teeth,
As she gorged in an unsightly manner.

9

A clapped-out old shag called Maree,
At a bar she was dying to wee.
In the face of the throng,
She wetted her thong,
Then pardoned foul wind to blow free.

10

A cashew on the end of one's dick,
Does not mean you've pulled a posh chick.
Barman Tam, he did shout,
"Scampi Fries have run out!"
Beryl then raged, "ah'll hae nuts thin ya prick!"

11

A bonny young quine in a frock,
Claimed an undying love for her Jock.
"You're just my kind of guy",
To which Jock did reply,
"a dae see ye sookin ma cock."

12

A benefit surfer called Drew,
With a list, that was headed, 'to-do'.
He'd wake long after dawn,
Give a fart, burp and yawn
And that day, fuck all else, would ensue.

13

The Trevi, a baroque masterpiece,
Only rivalled by marbles from Greece.
Arty summoned the strength,
He slipped in for a length,
To be plucked out, like a turd, by the police.

14

Richard was most aptly named
And with a neck very heavily veined.
His daily Yule log,
Would grace, some poor cunt's bog,
For blocked drains, he was quite often blamed.

Enuresis was a problem for Stan,
A strong kidney smelling young man.
His landlord called Briggs yelled,
"You must pay your digs!"
"Much ammonia?", Stan enquired from the can.

The McVee Family

16

Oppositional Defiance Disorder,
Means to not really do what you ought-a.
Take Tommy McVee,
He'd refuse to have tea,
But delighted in eating a snotter.

For young Tommy Tourette had a grip,
No joy in just shouting out flip.
He'd cunt, fuck and laugh,
And yell, "Miss, suck me aff!",
On his primary two summer trip.

Young Tom, with dog shit on his shoe,
Quite frankly did not have a clue.
Straight homeward he'd trudge,
With a boot caked in fudge,
His mum would have cleaning to do.

Tommy Snr. he felt some despair
And with a fart, from his chair, did declare;
"Efter seeventeen kids
And a life on the skids;
Cunt! That's it hen, we're no haen nae mair."

Entertainment, leisure and recreation

17

On a routine hand-party for Sam,
Involving five sisters and Palm.
With no nibbles required,
Sam had all he desired,
Including his favourite seat on the tram.

18

A sexual misfit called Dean,
He found plenty more fish on his screen.
To a pouting great cod,
He'd whack off his rod,
Then spatter Carp Monthly in cream.

19

A quiet, first date was the plan,
With her online, located new man.
Ethel's plans soon aborted,
So, with cum and drugs snorted,
Had group sex in the back of a van.

An online persona for Drew,
To be fair, in the main, was untrue.
"Girls know me as Chuck,
The prolific great fuck."
'Fact he lived, with his gran down in Crewe.

21

Big Henry was not very clean
And unconcerned with the need for hygiene.
His mum's tea towels stank,
From too many a wank,
But her cups had a beautiful sheen.

22

A young taxi driver named Hank,
'Tween fares was his habit to wank.
It became so damned drastic,
The seats required plastic,
But his spunk-covered taxi still stank.

23

A single, young woman from Poole,
Was quite often found as a rule;
With her fist up her bot
And a hand in her slot,
She missed her ex-boyfriend's huge tool.

24

A randy, old widow from Crieff,
Took a moment aside from her grief.
Asked a chap to her left,
"Do you like a loose cleft?"
Then she quickly removed her false teeth.

25

Morning PE with Joel Wikkes,
A post breakfast wank date for fat chicks.
His routine just started,
Poor Joey, he sharted,
A bidding war then ensued for his knicks.

A mucus-clogged Kenny when ten,
Amused friends when he laughed, now and then.
Chums' jaws soon did drop,
When snot bubbles went pop,
Leaving Kenny's face covered in phlegm.

The inevitable

27

Opening of a new sheltered housing complex

Hoping to smell just fresh paint,
Lady provost, she felt rather faint.
The huge fibre gel shot
Caused old Annie to trot;
Loose stool pong, greeted folks at the gate.

28

Recycling appealed to old Rose,
Ten bob for a kilo of clothes.
She filled several bags,
Full of shit laden rags,
Cashing in with a peg on her nose.

Auntie Floss came to afternoon tea,
With a toy dog, her baby, Enri.
The randy, gas-filled young Pug,
Stank the parlour with fug
And humped shins, much to everyone's glee.

Wednesday routine for old Fred,
Would see him tonking away in a shed.
"Nothing wrong," some might say,
"To pass the day in this way,"
But the garden store staff just saw red.

An incontinent lady called Trish,
She had problems controlling her pish.
Whenever she tippled,
Her whole bladder rippled,
Her drawers, ended up, fit for fish.

32

A cash grabbing teen called Denise,
By her husband, she was pre-deceased.
He was 96,
With a flaccid old dick
And by rule would be found underneath.

33

Young Knobby's old Gran, it was said,
Had not a solitary tooth in her head.
She'd fasten her gums,
Around Grandad's old plums
And suck them quite hard 'til they bled.

34

There was an old woman from Leeds,
Who choked down a large gob full of seed.
Her poor husband called Drew,
His lips would turn blue,
On account of his randy wife's deed.

35

There was an old man name of Jude,
At a wake, he behaved rather rude.
When quizzed, who was dead,
Just pan faced, he then said,
"Dunno, I'm just here for the food."

36

With advancing grey hair on her thatch,
Nan required a hair colour to match.
A pink rinse was found,
To improve her old mound,
But she still had a smelly old snatch.

37

An ageing sheep farmer from Arran,
With a sex life increasingly barren.
One day he was caught,
With his cock in a bott',
That belonged to an old ewe named Karen.

38

While disrobing one night for a kip,
Auld Boaby, yelled loudly, "Och, flip!"
When fumbling around,
In his trousers he found,
His cock was caught up in the zip.

39

Auld Boaby was famed as a rule,
For the size of his throbbing, great tool.
He'd receive frequent chants,
To display from his pants,
And obliging, he'd shake out his ghoul.

40

An anaemic old man name of Judd,
Had trouble obtaining 'nuff blood.
To bring to a rock,
His minuscule cock,
Which was often mistook for a fud.

41

An enuretic man not feeling champ',
Found his pyjamas increasingly damp.
His balls became sticky,
Along with his pricky,
His loins, they required, a revamp.

42

A saucy old bugger named Giles,
Whose sex life was ruined by piles.
His partner called Lear,
Pushed his knob in Giles' ear
And now once again, Giles-he smiles.

43

An ageing male actor in shades,
Retired to the damp everglades.
Where he and some pals,
Tickled each other's balls,
Whilst shouting abuse at the maids.

44

An old man from west Bangalore,
With an arse, running loose and quite sore.
He'd not been to Delhi,
But the gas in his belly,
Gave rise to concern there'd be more.

45

An old cock molester from Chester,
With a fetish for knick's polyester.
He'd eye up said togs,
In the gentlemen's bogs,
Then announce, hand outstretched, "I'm
Sylvester."

46

A frustrated, old man from Kent,
With a penis unfeasibly bent.
Making love was a chore
And left his wife wanting more,
For instead of just coming, he went.

Old Ethel looked into Pilates,
In a dress, she did not look too natty.
On attending she found,
Lardy arses abound,
Just a lame, token social for fatties.

A tired, old man on a bus,
Through discomfort, he loosened his truss.
But, out slipped his cock,
To a passenger's shock,
So, a handbag, he caught in the pus.

A randy, old priest called Tyrone,
Who sported a whopping great bone.
One day had it out,
Sister gave it a clout
And with pleasure, Tyrone, gave a groan.

50

There was an old lady from Poole,
Her sex life, to some, would seem cruel.
She'd go down on one knee,
For an aroused chimpanzee,
While being gored in the arse by a bull.

51

An old man, from the west isle of Muck,
With not one conventional fuck.
He'd eye up his flock
And while flicking his cock,
He yearned for some warm Peking duck.

52

A huge tattooed old lady from Rhyl,
She suffered from flesh overspill.
A tit-tat of Mons Meg,
Now hung down to her leg
And frankly was no longer brill'.

53

There was an old woman from Staines,
On her cunt she had massive chilblains.
Ablutions meant hell,
So, she'd quite often yell,
"Help! I'm pishing, like, broken glass panes."

54

A fragile, old couple from Stoke,
Planned one evening, to have a good poke.
'Twas too much for Miles,
When Fran punctured his piles,
Then with shock, she did suffer a stroke.

55

A buxom grandmother called Netta,
Oh boy! Could she fill out a sweater.
With prime juggs, big and round,
Invariably, she found,
Appreciation could not get much better.

Dysfunctional bowels, notable stools and flatulence frolics

56

A Saville Row tailor called Lear,
Touching cloth only filled him with fear.
The closet, you see,
Was up on floor three
And mostly engaged for the year.

57

Richard was most aptly named
And with a neck very heavily veined.
His daily Yule log,
Would grace, some poor cunt's bog,
For blocked drains, he was quite often blamed.

58

A lady from west Bangalore,
Dumped a pile of loose stools by her door.
A shocked passing crowd,
Heard her grunting out loud,
They all clapped and just shouted, "encore!"

59

An over-ripe lady called Tilly,
Wore knickers, all marked and not frilly.
She'd quite often wear,
More than several pair,
To put off her husband called Billy.

60

Colostomy Kate was a clart,
'Cause whenever she needed to fart;
She'd build up a whopper,
Then blow out the stopper,
The mess on the wall she'd call art.

61

A family's holiday plight,
By caravan, in Morecambe, o'er night.
Gran's incontinent bowel,
Had the place smelling foul,
As she 'lagered' the toilet with shite.

Rodger the Lodger

Grunting one out in the pan,
May not, always go, quite to plan.
Take for instance poor Rodger,
The impacted lodger,
Whose long johns were always stained tan.

Much fecal impaction for Rodge',
Was a draft that he just couldn't dodge.
He felt quite hard-pressed,
Of said stool, to divest,
Another log, he'd just failed, to dislodge.

Poor Rodge' thought he'd never feel light,
As he lay in a ward overnight.
Nurses' hearts were all bleeding,
As his body mass reading,
Showed 90% full of shite.

With contractions that came now and then,
The delivery came around ten.
With a triumphal shout,
Before his heart gave out,
He yelled, "slap it, and look after Ken."/

Ken was then in for the chop,
A crude method to flush such a plop.
Spare a thought for poor Rodge',
No more stools left to bodge,
His last motion had just faced the drop.

63

On safari with bad diarrhoea,
Caused by water that wouldn't run clear.
Johnny's shit splattered tent,
Required a large vent,
With his farting, no beasts would come near.

64

A plumber, he pushed with much might,
With a cleek on the blockage of shite.
He endeavoured to chop,
The gargantuan plop,
While the responsible party took flight.

65

An egg-bound old man, Ernest Motion,
Applied a great slap of hand lotion.
He called out very loud,
"my sphincter stands proud,
when it gives, I will cause a commotion."

66

An amorphous great mass name of Fran,
With laxity slammed, her big arse, on the pan.
Worms all curly and brown,
Then did sieve through her gown,
As she let go an over-baked flan.

Scatty Pete

A failing crowd pleaser called Pete,
Was promptly removed from the street.
To the children's delight,
He ate his own shite,
Whilst insisting, 'twas better than meat.

Pete was then shown to his room,
With a whack on his arse from a broom.
He cried, "Mum, you're unfair,
It was only a dare,"
She then yelled, "clean yer teeth, they're aw broon."

Pete replied, "My dear mum, I should mention
And I don't wish to add to your tension.
My teeth remain bright,
As I clean them with shite
See I do like to break with convention."

Pete was then huckled to bed,
With an arse that was tanned until red.
With a throbbing hot bum
And with homework undone,
He lay reading scat monthly instead.

68

As a precautionary measure strange Phil,
Concerned that he may become ill.
He'd check daily shits,
Along with his bits,
But be riled, the result, was a nil.

69

An anxious young man name of Robbie,
Would pace up and down in the lobby.
He'd yell, "please be fair,
You must let me in there,"
I'm about to push forth a large jobby.

70

On a foray one day in the wood,
The walker sighed loudly, "that's good."
A squat was a must,
And with one downward thrust,
Three kilos of digested food.

71

The escort just knew to make haste,
In swallowing down the love paste.
The drunk client had let off,
A loud trouser cough
And was about to eject some food waste.

72

A lad with a bag on his side,
He found it quite easy to hide.
Whenever 'twas full,
He would as a rule,
Empty the whole lot outside.

73

A lady was bothered with pains,
From throbbing, great varicose veins.
For support she wore tights,
Like solidified shites,
That resembled a route map of Spain.

74

There was a young man name of Howell,
Who unfortunately, was with collapsed bowel.
One day with the pastor,
He let go a plaster,
The pastor said, "Howell, that's foul."

75

A chap who would only eat millet,
Squatted down on a bucket to fill it.
He said, "I struggle to budge,
This impaction of fudge,
I'm egg bound and so just hope to will it."

Stan and Bertha

Bertha struggled with a chesty cough,
But her partner, he only could scoff.
Then with choking and gargling,
Leaving big Stanley marvelling,
A loud, trouser cough, she let off.

Bertha's rough meaty fart was a beezer,
When with passion, her Stan, went to squeeze
her.
With three coil shaped lumps,
Came more thunderous pumps,
He then rimmed her, the big diamond geezer.

77

An obsessional fellow called Jules,
Had a growing collection of stools.
Among the prized pieces,
Of catalogued faeces,
Were of Gran, armadillo and bull.

78

A lad from most Northern Gansu,
By his parents was named Sht-Pan Fu.
In the province, he'd be found,
Squatting close to the ground,
As for him any old place would do.

79

A flatulent man name of Bert,
Assumed the gas, that he passed, was inert.
When his trousers ignited,
A fire crew blue lighted,
But found Bert was no longer alert.

So, Duncan thought it'd be ace,
To fart in his sleeping mum's face.
Bad enough, you may think,
To cause such a stink,
But he sharted straight on her boat race.

An unfortunate fellow called Giles,
Yelled, "I'm flowing just like the Red Nile."
From the toilet he'd yell,
"I am bleeding like hell,
From these varicose veins on my piles."

Medical misdemeanours, disorders and enhancements

82

A transitioning man name of Pete,
Got surgeons to re-jig his meat.
A huge silicone pair,
Made everyone stare,
But the dead giveaway was his feet.

83

A man with a bowel infestation,
Caused medical staff much frustration.
He'd poke in his bed,
'Til his arsehole was red,
Then refuse to accept irrigation.

84

A filthy, old doctor named Crust,
Approached his large patient with lust.
He said, "I confess,
There's no need to undress,
But I would like to fondle your bust."

85

With an odour of rotting crustacean,
A man suffered alienation.
He'd scratch in his sleep,
For his flesh it did weep,
The result of a skin infestation.

86

A boy with a pus engorged head,
Gave a squeeze afore going to bed.
To the shock of his uncle,
He'd split a carbuncle
And grinning, he stood there and bled.

87

Surgical implant by knife,
Gave Knobby, new passion for life.
A very small dong,
Now some 12-inches long,
Put a smile on the face of his wife.

88

A bronchial man name of Hugh,
Had thick glossy sputum like glue.
He'd cough and he'd hack,
From a slap on the back,
By a large bosomed nurse dressed in blue.

89

A gargantuan cosmetic implant,
Was all that would satisfy Grant.
For a demanding young wife,
He'd go under the knife,
To resemble a bull elephant.

90

Nikola met with her surgeon,
"Nip 'n' tuck my big doss," she did urge him.
"My fur, it sits thick,
Like a caviar slick,
An' fir fuckin insult, I'm named after a fish!"

There was a young woman of Harrow,
Wot slid her cunt down on a marrow.
Medics had to exhume,
The great prize legume,
She then wheeled it straight home in a barrow.

Chelle

92

Halitosis was a problem for Chelle
And caused her breath to excessively smell.
Along with this challenge,
Was a pH imbalance,
Ensuring her fud stank as well.

With the breath of a monitor lizard
And oily scalp all druffed like a blizzard.
Chelle's hygiene not dandy,
She was far from eye candy,
With her slack warted dangly old gizzard.

Hospitality, food and drink

93

A penny tray sweetie piranha,
Was born into sugar Nirvana.
Her smile would cause grief,
With her puff candy teeth,
As she gorged in an unsightly manner.

94

A failing sous-chef, Gordon Bleu,
Unsurprisingly, had fuck all to do.
On one of many days off,
He'd rustle up scoff,
Some would say, from the sole of his shoe.

95

A cashew on the end of one's dick,
Does not mean you've pulled a posh chick.
Barman Tam, he did shout,
"Scampi Fries have run out!"
Beryl then raged, "ah'll hae nuts thin ya prick!"

At the fete, there were no great surprises,
Ethel's marrow took all the main prizes.
Wearing only sunscreen,
She was flicking her bean,
As she lay with the gourd 'tween her thizes.

Ken's Yule logs were bigger than most,
"I'm bunged up," he would commonly boast.
After days of inaction,
Caused by faecal impaction,
He'd see his friend off to the coast.

It was said that from dusk until dawn,
Mags would be fellated by Ron.
He had no sense of smell
And for him, just as well,
As her swollen old bean stank of prawn.

Young Todd pushed his wife to the brink,
Not only consumed by the drink.
In bed he would say,
To his wife's great dismay,
I can't choose on the brown or the pink.

100

A man with a case of trench foot,
Removed his large, rancid wet boot.
From his friends he took knocks,
For not changing his socks,
His feet, they looked like, boeuf en croute.

101

Poor hygiene was the problem with Frank,
Not accepting the claim that he stank.
With his hair full of grease
And a knob filled with cheese,
He applied for a job in a bank.

An overweight baker from Rhyl,
Who thought all of his products were brill.
To maintain a huge size,
He would eat all his pies
And in turn would just make himself ill.

A large man just sat fairly quiet,
By his wife, he'd been placed on a diet.
He had a strong hunch,
It was salad for lunch
And with tears in his eyes, he squeaked "fry it."

After several beakers of ale,
A man went incredibly pale.
His girlfriend then left,
With a hand on her cleft,
Shouting, "darling, tonight, you will fail!"

Filthy nails were the problem with Boothe,
In the mortuary the corpses were proof.
When preparing fresh food,
He was not very good,
Streptococci, au gratin de boeuf.

106

The booze got the better of Chris,
For a shot, he would swallow down Jiz.
Take a cock in his ear,
For a strong can of beer,
Then refute the fact he was pissed.

107

An undiscerning young man name of Cecil,
Adored his new girlfriend called Ethel.
She'd smoke in his car,
Scoff a deep-fried Mars bar
And for real she did hail from 'the Methil'.

108

Stavros's oversized daughter,
Would not really eat what she oughta.
For lunch she would grab,
A huge doner kebab,
Another poor lamb to the slaughter.

109

On the phone at five ordering the tea,
Between puffs, Franny hacked, "hecksquuuze me.
A hot dug fur the bairn;
Wan is long is ma airm,
An' a munch boax wi ketchup fur me."

110

A baker who hailed from Devizes
And responsible for local demizes.
His cooked meat, it would lay,
For way more than a day,
Then he'd slap it straight into his piezes.

A nursing home worker named Lorne,
Took his local real ale club by storm.
With beer branded, 'old toad'
And strong, 'eau d'commode',
A new age of appreciation was born.

112

A boy who had run out of sweets,
Would never succumb to defeat.
He'd throw his head back,
Then snort, gargle and hack,
And cough up, a soft warm, chewy treat.

113

A bowel test lab worker from Kent,
Repurposed shite kits that were spent.
The prod plastic stick,
Made a top-drawer toothpick,
No more lodged meaty chunks to torment.

Travel, Tourism and things International

114

On their hol's Ed and Flo felt dejected,
In the Hotel Dubai, quite neglected.
'Tween exotic birds sucking,
Noisy banging and fucking,
Not the calm desert break they'd expected.

115

Holiday plans for big Stan,
Essentially went down the pan.
On account of his weight,
He'd travel as freight
And on arrival, be transferred by van.

116

A man from Canton, called Lon Wei,
Suspected some mild tooth decay.
An orthodontist quite cute,
Asked which appointment might suit,
Lon simply replied, "two-thirty."

117

A huge smelly farmer from France,
Once took his old sow to a dance.
She was quite pleased at this,
But the cunt got so pissed,
She withered him up with a glance.

118

A man from Canton, Wan-Lon Pei,
To the toilet, he just had to flee.
He yelled, "my incontinence plight,
Stops me sleeping at night,
I'm ironically named, poor old me!"

119

A sickly, old tramp from Belize,
With hairy bits covered in fleas.
In the street he would beg,
With a gangrenous leg,
Sending passers-by off with a wheeze.

On a passenger flight to Milan,
There was an enormous-arsed man.
The air grew quite thick,
Making cabin crew sick,
When he dumped a large stool in the pan.

121

There once was a man from Nepal,
With a penis just rather too small.
His partner called Keashur,
From his cock got no pleasure,
So, he shagged him all night with his balls.

122

A sensitive girl from Frankfurt,
With large hairy nipples, quite pert.
From her Mann just one tweak,
Would remain erect for a week,
And she took the next size in a shirt.

123

A pained, Oober driver named Reg,
Would give himself pleasure with veg.
Once driving a taxi,
With a yam in his jaxi,
He drove his Prius into a hedge.

124

In a corner of Uzbekistan,
Lived a famous emphysemic young man.
He coughed into a jar,
Heavy lumps of catarrh,
Then filled the holes in the side of his van.

125

A ninety a day man called Keith,
For his hol's, he would choose Tenerife.
Despite travelling afar,
He just sat at the bar,
Arriving home with a tan on his teeth.

A tall, busty girl from Milan,
Was approached by a short-arsed young man.
He said, "I beseech,
These fake tits, I can't reach,
So, I'll settle for fisting your nan."

(translation)

Una ragazza tettona alta da Milano,
È stato avvicinato da un giovane sono breve.
Ha detto che vi prego,
Queste tette rifatte, non riesco a raggiungere,
Così mi accontento di fisting il nan.

(For the more educated aficionado)

(re-translated from Italian)

A busty girl high from Milan,
He was approached by a young are short.
He said, "please,
These boob job, I can't get to,
So, I'll settle for fisting the nan."

Luton Bert

A customs official named Bert,
To a bag he became quite alert.
While she seemed within limits,
Bert said, "hang on one minute,
what are these lumps in your shirt?"

Bert, was then called by his boss,
A customs ball breaker named Floss.
She said, "Bert, I insist,
that my help you enlist,
as we may have to check out her doss."

Floss she then eyed up the knit,
Before closely inspecting the clit.
Floss then said, "oh, my, word
that is never a burd,
Bert! Check-out, what we once thought was tit."

Bert, he then lunged at the swellings,
As to what was in there was no telling.
He then locks on his mitts,
To the once proclaimed tits
And in shock, he began to start yelling…/

Bert then cried loudly, "Oh, wow!"
I don't know for why or for how.
From the swollen great pair,
Came-forth three puppies fair,
A labradoodle, a pug and a chow.

The smuggler turned out to be Ray,
A cross dresser, from Luton, by day.
He'd smuggle small dugs,
From within his fake juggs,
In a bid just to eke out his pay.

For Bert there was only promotion,
A facemask, some gloves and hand lotion.
Instead of frisking for pugs,
He had to pluck drugs,
From a trafficker's 9-inch-long motion.

A rich tapestry of the human condition

128

An overzealous PT name of Trotter,
She never made time just to potter.
Her cunt it would drool,
En-route home, from the school,
Thinking of, simply huge, unmarked jotters.

129

The irascible girlfriend of Bob,
Condemnation just flew from her gob.
His jokes they would flounder,
He'd tiptoe around her,
Another two weeks on the blob.

130

A young gender fuck up named Troy,
Was anatomically born as a boy.
He would oft' dress in blue,
Took size ten in a shoe
And the sight of big juggs gave him joy.

In Cambridgeshire down by a bank,
Sat a lady whose fanny just stank.
A cunt from a punt shouted,
"show us some front!"
She yelled, "no, I don't dare, it's too rank!"

132

A man who was partially blind,
He grabbed a large woman's behind.
He said, "pardon my dear,
May I use you to steer
And oh boy! you are overdesigned."

133

A pious old cunt, Walter Clarke,
Whose bite was as bad as his bark.
He'd enter a room,
With no va-va-voom,
He was lacking a true vital spark.

134

A man of the cloth from a priory,
His physique, some would say, was quite wiry.
Invitations to tea,
Never filled him with glee,
He'd consult his oft' fully booked diary.

135

The modest abode of skint Martin,
Was mainly described as 'quite Spartan'.
He found it a pain,
With not a thread to his name,
He'd neither pot, to piss in, or fart in.

136

A blood filled, thick blue veined large cock,
Hung down from the kilt of big Jock.
He denied women thrills,
Keeping out winter chills,
As he tucked the beast into his sock.

137

A 'jist eet', car driver called Tel',
His car did excessively smell.
Bad driving and breaking,
Reduced the night's takings,
With pizza smashed in his foot well.

138

There once was a woman of Stroud,
Accused by many, of coming, out loud.
To her beau, she'd implore,
"Please don't slam my back door,
Shut it gently, to just please the crowd."

139

A deluded young man got a clout,
When his aunt caught him thumping one out.
He yelled, "I'm not that mean,
When you're flicking your bean,
You continue and give me a pout!"

140

A serial philanderer from Fife,
Had been shagging some bird, not his wife.
He enjoyed a good blow
And let flings come and go,
With not a word to his trouble and strife.

141

On applying emollient cream,
Fat Stanley was chafing his dream.
For the Iron Man event,
He'd emerge from the tent,
Having breakfasted well, it would seem.

142

An eloquent girl feeling rough,
Who really did feel, quite the scruff.
Announced with great savoir faire,
"I'll shave bodily hair,
but will leave my luxuriant muff."

A tidy young lad name of Pete,
Was constantly pounding his meat.
He'd use only his thumbs,
To make himself cum,
Then fold up his tum wipe quite neat.

A peerage for some I'd bemoan,
An inheritance, for no work of their own.
Take Lord Wallop of Thane,
Who'd announce under pain,
"this bad donkey is just out on loan."

A cock heavy laddie called Blair,
Felt his gagging young lass gasp for air.
She'd brought to a rock,
His non-standard cock,
Blair then leered, "swallow more if you dare."

146

A bonny young quine in a frock,
Claimed an undying love for her Jock.
"You're just my kind of guy",
To which Jock did reply,
"a dae see ye sookin ma cock."

147

A cricket fanatic called Nat,
On his cock, he had tattooed a bat.
Eyeing up his wife's crease,
That he'd suitably greased
And with one forward lunge yelled, "howzatt!"

148

So, GRINDR, appealed to fat Stan,
No problem in getting his man.
With copious hair
And a fart like a bear,
Drooling suitors, arrived soon, by van.

149

A benefit surfer called Drew,
With a list, that was headed, 'to-do',
He'd wake long after dawn,
Give a fart, burp and yawn
And that day, fuck all else, would ensue.

150

With a large disposable income,
Roddy grinned and exclaimed, "I'm fair dinkum."
Between labels and status
And no forthcoming hiatus,
He skipped off to the pub for some drinkums.

151

Lockdown was 'nae bother' for Tam,
"Fuck yer face masks, a dae give a damn."
Daily he would get sloshed
And his hands went unwashed,
Proving he was forever 'the bam'!

152

A doting hip father got cross,
At his naughty young son, he called Ross.
"It's chai latte," Ross beamed,
But all was not, what it seemed,
As instead of soy' milk, he'd used gloss.

153

A virtue-signalling twat,
Kept true thoughts firmly under their hat.
"...which religious persuasion,
will further my station,
and for whom is the best side to bat?"

154

With a blockage in his mum's chimney flue
And fire-starting about to ensue.
For naughty young Ben,
Who loved uniformed men,
What else was the young lad to do.

155

A huge, lazy bastard called James,
Refused to take part in school games.
With no kit for sports,
N' made to wear, 'the' school shorts,
He was forced to partake with pish stains.

156

In a cacophony of gargling phlegm,
Fag-ash-Lil caught a breath now and then.
With digits of yellow
And a voice not too mellow,
Numbered days, just a matter of when.

157

A Parisian fellow quite meek,
Who'd not wanked in almost a week.
On thrashing his tool,
He caused such a pool,
His bonne femme, clapped and yelled
"magnifique!"

158

A clapped-out, old shag called Maree,
At a bar she was dying to wee.
In the face of the throng,
She wetted her thong,
Then pardoned foul wind to blow free.

159

Enuresis was a problem for Stan,
A strong kidney smelling young man.
His landlord called Briggs yelled,
"you must pay your digs!"
"Much ammonia?", Stan enquired from the can.

160

In order to have restful sleep,
The young lady, her hands, she would keep.
Clasped firm to her cunt,
She'd throw in the odd shunt
And while coming, her knees went quite weak.

With rotting great fat plates of meat,
Bob was formerly proud of his feet.
Now with cuticle fails
And puff pastry toenails,
His podiatrist succumbed to defeat.

Arty and Fanny

162

More than once at a rugby club party,
The chaps would become rather clarty.
A particular fool,
Was found dangling his jewel,
Down the throat of a centre called Arty.

Arty's Valentine morn' was a battle,
Tarnished by his now usual old prattle.
Growing tired of his patter,
Fanny shut down his natter
And exclaimed, "you're no' getting a rattle."

Arty and Fanny were flittin,
The old house, they were finally quittin.
A' went up in a puff,
Said, "it's maistly your stuff,
So the coast o' the flit am no splittin."

The Trevi, a baroque masterpiece,
Only rivalled by marbles from Greece.
Arty summoned the strength,
He slipped in for a length,
To be plucked out, like a turd, by the police.

163

An antisocial young lady called Bex,
Engaged daily in loud tantric sex.
Demonstrating no shame,
Whether on bus, car or plane,
She caused fellow travellers to vex.

164

The girlfriend of Miles while in bed,
Would give him much pleasure with head.
On offloading Jiz,
She grew bored with this,
So, she pissed on his body instead.

165

An embarrassing feature of Frank,
Was that with, every wink, he would wank.
The problem was this,
His left eye was amiss,
Poked out by a stick in a prank.

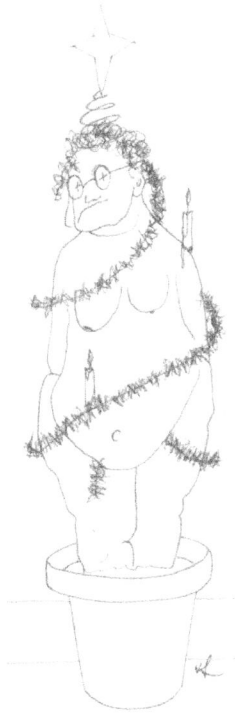

166

Yuletide celebrations for Knobby,
Saw him find a fresh theme for a body.
His embalmed great grandmother,
Had one use or another,
Was found dressed as a tree in the lobby.

167

There was a young lady called Tess,
Who turned out in a bit of a mess.
Her beau she called Billy,
Shot a load from his willie,
All over her new party dress.

168

An ageing plump lady from Ayr,
With thick, bushy grey, pubic hair.
For young men in the street,
She would happily greet,
Saying "Come have a feel if you dare."

169

Something unique about Neve,
She had a cunt like a sorcerer's sleeve.
Local press once did boast,
"This girl's cunt's like a close!"
That left our poor Nevey, quite peeved.

A raven-haired girl from Nantucket,
Her big mound, she decided to pluck it.
The fur round her clit,
Just grew thick as shit,
So she managed to fill a large bucket.

171

Big Stanley stood glued to the spot,
With his partner's large cock up his bot.
Big Chucky you see,
Had decided to pee,
Stanley thought, Chucky'd chucked a whole lot.

172

A horny young man called Fabrice,
He would swallow down cock, just to please.
From his partner called Kurt,
He'd gulp down a great squirt
And then empty his balls with a squeeze.

173

Big Stanley would often lament,
"My love club it is twisted and bent!"
He had little remorse,
'Bout being hung, like a horse,
Avid suitors would often relent.

174

A man with a massive dysfunction,
Was proud of his meaty, love truncheon.
His girlfriend called Red,
Would give him great head
And swallow it down for her luncheon.

175

A tall buxom woman called Tess,
Would quite often loosen her dress.
From udder to udder,
She'd wobble and judder,
Leaving women and men in distress.

176

A MILF with a slack hairy fud,
Insisted she shop semi-scud.
Viewing close from the ground.
A young shelf-stacker found,
His cock had a full rush of blood.

177

An incontinent man from Tiree,
With problems controlling his wee.
His sloppy great peg,
Would slap off his leg,
His wellingtons filled to the knee.

178

To the prison, the young man was led,
By a guard, he was shown to his bed.
The large cellmate then sneered,
"I prefer a smooth beard!"
And grinning, he'd pat the lad's head.

A mortuary worker named Dot,
Was immediately sacked on the spot.
To her boss' dismay,
Things went missing each day,
A home search found Dot, had the lot.

Mortimer Cream, who was not at all well,
Entered into a marriage of hell.
His husband called Tim,
Took the chance of a rim,
Then loudly complained of the smell.

On an outing one-day to the pool,
Young Tommy was playing the fool.
Too close to the wash,
He fell in with a splosh
And floated around like a stool.

182

A numerical lush hailed from Leith,
Re consumption would lie through his teeth.
He'd insist school night drinking,
Aided lateral thinking,
Then called out, "mine's a double please chief."

183

A glorious maid from a village,
Who was loaded with wonderful spillage.
A new bra, it would creak,
In much less than a week,
On account of abundance of fillage.

A young air-steward, who said, "call me Rae,"
Quite simply had too much to say.
With his petulant fluffing,
He required a good stuffing,
On a passenger flight from Beauvais.

185

An Oxfordshire lady called Fi,
Stood proud by the river to wee.
A swift passing punt,
Flicked an oar off her cunt,
That made her grimace on one knee.

186

A fickle young man named Pete,
Would essentially vote with his feet,
He'd shag many old nags,
Just to empty his bags,
Then announce, "my work here is complete."

Coco

187

A night support worker called Colin,
Was in for a really hard ballin'.
His charge lay on the floor,
As Col'n smoked by the door,
Hours before, the poor cunt had fallen.

On the Monday, wee Coco felt spent,
To his boss he did try to lament.
"Al no smoke onnymair,
Al vape oan the stair
And puff the hail time jist fur Lent!"

Before Colin was sent on his way,
His boss said, "Ave jist wan thing tae say,
Tak ma candy floss oil,
Yais it quick 'cos it spoils,
Geeze yer fags Col'n and have a nice day."

Bussing home, wee Coco felt sad,
He could only just think he'd been had.
Due to his inaction,
His charge lay in traction
And he knew the floss oil would taste bad.

Costa Del Far

188

An early-retired tour de force,
With self-praise he was left feeling hoarse.
Ruined lives in his wake,
Not his only mistake
And no stranger to the courts of divorce.

Reinventing in circ's quite bizarre,
He retired to the Costa Del Far.
A new bride by his side,
He'd take for a ride,
Until he could source a new star.

The problem existing you see,
The new bride was an ex-employee.
She was sacked/- reinstated,
On a proviso she dated,
Bed and board in her home was her fee.

This man's future remains with the gods,
With morality, he is at close odds.
Along with bent peers,
He looks back and leers,
He's up there with the worst of all sods.

189

A former care worker called Mae,
Sang like a canary one day.
Gaining over exposure,
By her protected disclosure,
HR then ensured she would pay.

190

A paid academic called Tim,
Whose wallet was filled to the brim.
He'd turn a blind eye,
To malfeasance and lies,
Then give the head honcho a rim.

191

At a specially held case review,
The outcome surprised very few.
'We have thrown out concerns,
But have lessons to learn'.
Rhetoric that wad mak a sow spew.

Oh Joy!

192

A man guilty of ill-judged decisions,
Approached staff with disdain and derision.
A photostat of his cock,
Not contained by a sock,
Forced his job to be under revision.

Resignation was duly accepted,
Injured parties were left quite affected.
Registration intact,
The forthcoming fact,
Was promotion and issues deflected.

This greatly indulged sex offender,
Was to add to the standards agenda.
His transferable skills,
Of faxing cheap thrills,
Saw him as a public body new member.

With several years in his post,
Colleagues raised him a glass in a toast.
On the gravy express,
A new post to contest,
His offending a forgotten past ghost.

193

A bent chief exec small and plug,
Had everyone down as a mug.
With neglect he was riddled
and felt rules should be fiddled,
He retired with his cheque looking smug.

194

Familiar with GDPR?
Most bent cunts, they usually are.
To hide omission and shite,
They use great legal might
And keep a tight lid on their jar.

195

Limerick work once completed,
Should see no good foray deleted.
The prose, they must rhyme,
Showing wit, some sublime
And beg the question, whether one, be repeated.

Postscript

Faced with a doss like a slaughterhouse skip,
The surgeon, he commented "flip!"
Colleagues muttered "good heavens,
Cor blimey and crivvens,
This needs more than a tuck and a nip."

List of Limericks by first line, following on from 'Executive Summary'…

16. Oppositional Defiance Disorder,
17. On a routine hand-party for Sam,
18. A sexual misfit called Dean,
19. A quiet, first date was the plan,
20. An online persona for Drew,
21. Big Henry was not very clean,
22. A young taxi driver named Hank,
23. A single young woman from Poole,
24. A randy, old widow from Crieff,
25. Morning PE with Joel Wikkes,
26. A mucus-clogged Kenny when ten,
27. Hoping to smell just fresh paint,
28. Recycling appealed to old Rose,
29. Auntie Floss came to afternoon tca,
30. Wednesday routine for old Fred,
31. An incontinent lady called Trish,
32. A cash grabbing teen called Denise,
33. Young Knobby's old Gran, it was said,
34. There was an old woman from Leeds,
35. There was an old man name of Jude,
36. With advancing grey hair on her snatch,
37. An ageing sheep farmer from Arran,
38. While disrobing one night for a kip,
39. Auld Boaby was famed as a rule,
40. An anaemic old man name of Judd,
41. An enuretic man not feeling champ',
42. A saucy old bugger named Giles,
43. An ageing male actor in shades,

44. An old man from west Bangalore,
45. An old cock molester from Chester,
46. A frustrated, old man from Kent,
47. Old Ethel looked into Pilates,
48. A tired, old man on a bus,
49. A randy, old priest called Tyrone,
50. There was an old lady from Poole,
51. An old man, from the west isle of Muck,
52. A huge tattooed old lady from Rhyl,
53. There was an old woman from Staines,
54. A fragile, old couple from Stoke,
55. A buxom grandmother called Netta,
56. A Saville Row tailor called Lear,
57. Richard was most aptly named,
58. A lady from west Bangalore,
59. An over-ripe lady called Tilly,
60. Colostomy Kate was a clart,
61. A family's holiday plight,
62. Grunting one out in the pan,
63. On safari with bad diarrhoea,
64. A plumber, he pushed with much might,
65. An egg-bound old man, Ernest Motion,
66. An amorphous great mass name of Fran,
67. A failing crowd pleaser called Pete,
68. As a precautionary measure strange Phil,
69. An anxious young man name of Robbie,
70. On a foray one day in the wood,
71. The escort just knew to make haste,
72. A lad with a bag on his side,
73. A lady was bothered with pains,

74. There was a young man name of Howell,
75. A chap who would only eat millet,
76. Bertha struggled with a chesty cough,
77. An obsessional fellow called Jules,
78. A lad from most Northern Gansu,
79. A flatulent man name of Bert,
80. So Duncan thought it'd be ace,
81. An unfortunate fellow called Giles,
82. A transitioning man name of Pete,
83. A man with a bowel infestation,
84. A filthy old doctor named Crust,
85. With an odour of rotting crustacean,
86. A boy with a pus engorged head,
87. Surgical implant by knife,
88. A bronchial man name of Hugh,
89. A gargantuan cosmetic implant,
90. Nikola met with her surgeon,
91. There was a young woman from Harrow,
92. Halitosis was a problem for Chelle,
93. A penny tray sweetie piranha,
94. A failing sous-chef, Gordon Bleu,
95. A cashew on the end of one's dick,
96. At the fete, there were no great surprises,
97. Ken's Yule logs were bigger than most,
98. It was said that from dusk until dawn,
99. Young Todd pushed his wife to the brink,
100. A man with a case of trench foot,
101. Poor hygiene was the problem with Frank,
102. An overweight baker from Rhyl,
103. A large man just sat fairly quiet,

104. After several beakers of ale,
105. Filthy nails were the problem with Boothe,
106. The booze got the better of Chris,
107. An undiscerning young man name of Cecil,
108. Stavros's oversized daughter,
109. On the phone at five ordering the tea,
110. A baker who hailed from Devizes,
111. A nursing home worker named Lorne,
112. A boy who had run out of sweets,
113. A bowel test lab worker from Kent,
114. On their hol's Ed and Flow felt dejected,
115. Holiday plans for big Stan,
116. A man from Canton, called Lon Wei,
117. A huge smelly farmer from France,
118. A man from Canton, Wan-Lon Pei,
119. A sickly old tramp from Belize,
120. On a passenger flight to Milan,
121. There once was a man from Nepal,
122. A sensitive girl from Frankfurt,
123. A pained, Oober driver called Reg,
124. In a corner of Uzbekistan,
125. A ninety a day man called Keith,
126. A tall, busty girl from Milan,
127. A customs official named Bert,
128. An overzealous PT name of Trotter,
129. The irascible girlfriend of Bob,
130. A young gender fuck up named Troy,
131. In Cambridgeshire down by a bank,
132. A man who was partially blind,
133. A pious old cunt, Walter Clarke,
134. A man of the cloth from a priory,

135. The modest abode of skint Martin,
136. A blood filled, thick blue veined large cock,
137. A 'jist eet', car driver called Tel',
138. There once was a woman of Stroud,
139. A deluded young man got a clout,
140. A serial philanderer from Fife,
141. On applying emollient cream,
142. An eloquent girl feeling rough,
143. A tidy young lad name of Pete,
144. A peerage for some I'd bemoan,
145. A cock heavy laddie called Blair,
146. A bonny young quine in a frock,
147. A cricket fanatic called Nat,
148. So, GRINDR, appealed to fat Stan,
149. A benefit surfer called Drew,
150. With a large disposable income,
151. Lockdown was 'nae bother' for Tam,
152. A doting hip father got cross,
153. A virtue-signalling twat,
154. With a blockage in his mum's chimney flue,
155. A huge, lazy bastard called James,
156. In a cacophony of gargling phlegm,
157. A Parisian fellow quite meek,
158. A clapped-out, old shag called Maree,
159. Enuresis was a problem for Stan,
160. In order to have restful sleep,
161. With rotting great fat plates of meat,
162. More than once at a rugby club party,
163. An antisocial young lady called Bex,
164. The girlfriend of Miles while in bed,
165. An embarrassing feature of Frank,

166. Yuletide celebrations for Knobby,
167. There was a young lady called Tess,
168. An ageing plump lady from Ayr,
169. Something unique about Neve,
170. A raven-haired girl from Nantucket,
171. Big Stanley stood glued to the spot,
172. A horny young man called Fabrice,
173. Big Stanley would often lament,
174. A man with a massive dysfunction,
175. A tall buxom woman called Tess,
176. A MILF with a slack hairy fud,
177. An incontinent man from Tiree,
178. To the prison, the young man was led,
179. A mortuary worker named Dot,
180. Mortimer Cream, who was not at all well,
181. On an outing one-day to the pool,
182. A numerical lush hailed from Leith,
183. A glorious maid from a village,
184. A young air-steward who said "call me Rae,"
185. An Oxfordshire lady called Fi,
186. A fickle young man named Pete,
187. A night support worker called Colin,
188. An early-retired tour de force,
189. A former care worker called Mae,
190. A paid academic called Tim,
191. At a specially held case review,
192. A man guilty of ill-judged decisions,
193. A bent chief exec small and plug,
194. Familiar with GDPR?
195. Limerick work once completed,

P.S. Faced with a doss like a slaughterhouse skip,

A Gripping Read
*****

(Some hilarious views of peristalsis outcomes from an affliction perspective set into the most sublime of prose. A joy to read while dropping a couple of six-inch coils)
Dr. Todd Baker, MGBGT, Resident Academic of The Hamilton Institute into Flatulence Research, New Delhi
*****

(I agree, a veritable 5 chocolate star body of work)
Steven Fries
*****

(Cheeky Bastard)
Stan and Bertha Slackbottom, Staines
*****

(I emphatically deny any wrongdoing)
Lord Wallop of Thane
*****

(I'll sue)
Nikola Snapper, Troon
*****

(Phone me!)
Dr Allison Rummage. CBT Counsellor

Printed in Great Britain
by Amazon